PLENTY OF LOVE TO GO ROUND!

Emma Chichester Clark

JONATHAN CAPE
LONDON

For my young
and beautiful
grandma

Emma Chichester Clark began the website **Plumdog Blog** in 2012,
chronicling the real-life adventures of her lovable "whoosell"
(whippet, Jack Russell and poodle cross) Plum. Emma soon
gained thousands of loyal Plumdog devotees, and in 2014 a book
of the blog was published by Jonathan Cape. This picture book
story is the second Plumdog book for children following
Love is My Favourite Thing.

First published 2016
001

Copyright © Emma Chichester Clark, 2016
The moral right of the author has been asserted

Printed in China
A CIP catalogue record for this book is available from the British Library

ISBN: 978–0–857–55123–8

All correspondence to:
Jonathan Cape, Penguin Random House Children's,
80 Strand, London WC2R 0RL

MIX
Paper from
responsible sources
FSC® C018179
FSC
www.fsc.org

I AM PLUM.

I am a one and only special Plum.

I live with Emma and Rupert. They are my mummy and daddy.

They say I am their Special One.

My best friends are Sam and Gracie who live next door, and I am also their best and only one.

But one day, Gracie said, "We've got a surprise for you, Plum!"

"This is Binky!"
said Sam.

He was holding
a cat.

I am not keen on cats.

"He loves you, Plum! Don't you LOVE him?" asked Gracie.
"We love him!" said Sam.

At least in the park, I could try to forget him.
The park is for dogs. It's for me and my friends.

"I say!" said Esther.
"Is that cat with you?"

I couldn't believe it!

"Who's your new friend?" asked Rocket.
"He's not my friend – he's nothing
to do with me!" I said.

"Well, he's following you!" said Bean.

"Go home!" I said.

When I got home, he was there — in my garden. "It's nice to have a cat around," said Emma.

No! It isn't! It isn't!

He followed me everywhere,

sniffed where I sniffed,

rolled where I rolled,

peed when I peed,

stretched when
I stretched.

I couldn't
get away
from him.

The only safe place was the shed.

But the cat came in. "Miaow!" he said...

...and the door slammed shut! I was stuck with the cat.

"Miaow!"
he said, and
off he went.

"CATS!" I thought.
Now no one
will find me.

They might not
remember me ...
Who will feed me?

But I was wrong
about that because
Binky came back. He
brought Sam and Gracie.

"Silly old Plum!"
said Gracie.

"Binky saved you!"
said Sam.

They told Emma
and my daddy.
"Clever Binky!"
said my daddy.

"He's SO clever!"
said Sam.

He's a CAT! Just a cat —
nothing special about it.

"Oh, look at Binky!"
said Gracie as he
ran up a tree.

"He can do **anything!**"
said Sam.

It's true. It's really
true, I thought.

They thought he was wonderful, whatever he did. He was the new Special One.

I thought he was a show off, clever-clogs cat.

"He's ruining everything, Esther," I said. "What can I do?"

"Have you tried being friends?" asked Jakey.

"Yes, that's a good idea," said Esther.

"I can't be friends with a cat!" I told Bean.

"What if they love the cat more than me?" I asked Rocket.

"Oh, there's plenty of love to go round," he said.

So I went round to
Sam and Gracie.

They were watching TV.
The cat was outside.

He came
back when
he saw me.

So I pushed the door shut and leant against the cat flap.

"You can stay out!" I told him...

"Stay out till I say so."

It started to rain but I guarded the door, and then I felt awful. He may be a cat but he was still a little creature and we're all little creatures that need to be loved.

Just then,
Emma and my
daddy came.

They saw
little Binky,

and then
they saw me.

They knew
what I'd done.

They brought
Binky in.
"Oh, poor Binky!"
said Grace.

"Why didn't he
come through
the cat flap?"
asked Sam.

I looked at
Emma and she
looked at me.

"Now, Plummie," she said. "You'll always be special. You're my Special One... but you are going to have to put up with the cat!

There's room in our hearts for him, and for YOU!"

"You've got a big heart, haven't you, Plummie?" said Emma.

And suddenly I could feel it growing. It grew BIGGER and BIGGER.

Luckily, my bed was big enough too –
for two little creatures.
And what Rocket said is true –
it's really true...

...there's PLENTY of love
to go round and round.
There's plenty of love to go round.